Drum Beats

Sharon M. Draper

SCHOLASTIC INC.
New York Toronto London Auckland Sydney
Mexico City New Delhi Hong Kong Buenos Aires

Cover illustration and interior illustrations by Charlene Potts

Printed in the U.S.A.

ISBN 0-439-57674-1

1 2 3 4 5 6 7 8 9 10 40 12 11 10 09 08 07 06 05 04 03

Contents

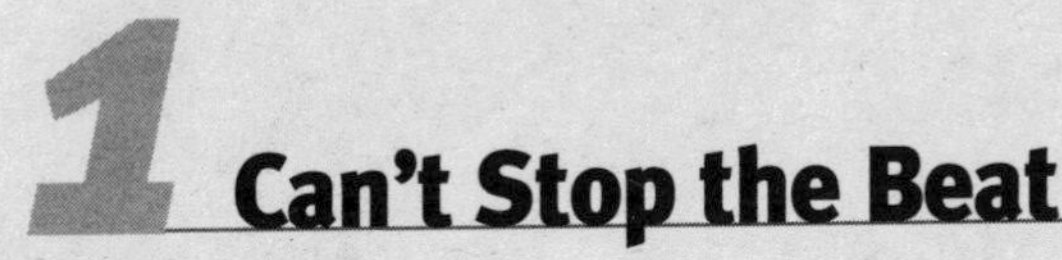

1 Can't Stop the Beat

"Tonya, stop that!"

Ms. Kane, my English teacher, had stopped class to yell at me.

"Stop what?" I asked.

"You know what I'm talking about," Ms. Kane said.

I could tell she was getting mad.

"Stop that noise!"

I really didn't know what she was talking about. "Stop what noise, Ms. Kane?"

"Stop that rapping on your desk with your pencil!"

I looked down at my pencil. I had been tapping out a beat on my desk. I do it all the time. I never think about it—I just like to beat

out rhythms.

"I'm sorry, Ms. Kane," I told her. "I can't help it. My pencil hears the music in my head, and it just has to tap it out!"

"Well, tell your pencil to tap someplace else!" Ms. Kane said. "It gets on my nerves. And you're distracting the class."

I gave her the look you give teachers when they're being unreasonable, but I put my pencil down. She was talking about nouns and verbs, but I wasn't listening very well. I was thinking about a song I had heard on the radio last night. It had a loud bass beat.

My mind left the verbs on Ms. Kane's blackboard and jumped back to the beats of that song. I started tapping with my fingers to the rhythm. Tap-Tap. Tap-Tap-Tap. Tap.

"Tonya! I said stop that!" Ms. Kane yelled again.

"OK! OK!" I yelled back. "I'm sorry!"

I rolled my hands into fists and put them on my lap. I tried very hard to pay attention and stop tapping. But it wasn't easy.

"Get your pencils out, class," Ms. Kane said.

"Do questions one to ten in your notebook."

I gave her my crazy look again. If she doesn't want me to tap a beat with my pencil, why does she tell me to pick it up? Pencils were never made for writing. Pencils were made for tapping out a cool beat. So were pens, and fingertips, and even sticks I find in the street.

I did question number one. I did question number two. But then the music in my head returned. It was louder than before. It was louder than the verbs on that page.

I started to whisper the words to the beat I heard. Bop-de-bop-bop-bop. Ta-dop. Ta-bop. Ta-dop. Ta-bop. I forgot all about question number three. My pencil kept the rhythm with the beats that I made: Bop-de-bop-bop-bop. Ta-dop. Ta-bop. Ta-dop. Ta-bop.

The classroom was very quiet, except for me whispering to myself and beating out the rhythms on my desk. I didn't notice the other kids giggling. I didn't notice the teacher walking toward me.

"Tonya!" she yelled. She was standing right by my desk.

I jumped when she called my name. The rest of the class laughed.

"Please stay after class, Tonya. We have a problem."

The bell rang, and I slumped in my seat. Everyone else laughed and ran out of the room.

If you were Ms. Kane, what would you say to Tonya?

2 All Tapped Out

"Do you like music, Tonya?" Ms. Kane asked.

"I like it a whole lot better than I like verbs," I told her.

"Do you see how your rapping and tapping is a problem in class?" she asked.

"I guess I can see how it's a problem for you," I said. "But it makes me happy. I really do try to stop, Ms. Kane, but I can't help it."

"Are you in the band here at school?" she asked me.

"No, my mother said I couldn't take band. I'm in the choir instead."

"Can you sing?"

"Not a bit. I sound like a crow!"

Ms. Kane laughed. "So why don't you change to the band class. You need to learn to play the drums."

"My mother said girls shouldn't play the drums. She said they are too heavy to carry and are not very lady-like. And she said they make too much noise."

"Does your mother know how much you beat the drums on books and desks and chairs?"

"I guess so. Ever since I was a little girl, I've liked to hit on things and make noise. I used to turn waste baskets upside down so I could bop on the bottom of them."

"Did you empty them first?" Ms. Kane asked.

"No, I just took my waste basket drum and left the mess on the floor. It always made my mother mad. I made drums out of everything—oatmeal boxes, the kitchen table, even the top of the toilet! It's not just you, Ms. Kane. I think I drive my mother crazy, too."

"Is that why you're not in the band?"

"My mother told me to learn to sing and

stop hitting on stuff all the time. She yells at me just like you do," I told her.

"I'm sorry I yelled at you, Tonya," Ms. Kane said, "but we have to find a cure for your drumming fingers."

"I'm sorry, too, Ms. Kane," I said. "I'll try very hard to stop doing that. I promise."

"Thanks, Tonya. Now get to your next class."

I ran out of the room and down the hall. My friend Jackie waited for me. "What did she want?" Jackie asked.

"She says I'm so smart I should stay home tomorrow because I already know everything in the world!"

Jackie and I laughed as we ran to math class. I like math. You can get some good sounds out of a ruler tapped on the side of a desk.

How would you describe Tonya?

3 Pick Up Sticks

After lunch I had my music class. That class is fun because the teacher, Mr. Smith, plays all types of music for us. Sometimes we hear oldies, or country songs, or even opera music. I get to beat on my desk as much as I want. The only bad part about the class is that I have to sing. I try to sing very quietly so no one can hear me. Sometimes I just move my mouth and pretend. When I sing loudly, everyone gives me funny looks. I sound like a squeaky door.

Mr. Smith walked into class holding some papers in his hand.

"I have the papers for the music contest next week," he said. "If anyone would like to enter the contest, the first prize is one hundred dollars!"

"One hundred dollars!" we all yelled.

That was a lot of money. Everyone wanted to enter the contest.

"What do you have to do to win?" I asked Mr. Smith.

"You have to sing like a bird!" he said and laughed.

"I sing like a duck. A duck is a bird. Does that count?" I asked with a grin.

Mr. Smith liked me even though I could not sing. He liked me because I loved music. It was not my fault I couldn't sing.

"Maybe not for this contest," he said.

Jackie took an entry form for the contest. She really does sing like a bird—one of those pretty birds that sings in the summer sunshine.

Leo took an entry form too. His voice sounds like smooth candy when he sings.

A couple of other kids also wanted to try for the contest. Mr. Smith had one last sheet of paper in his hand.

"Tonya?" he said to me. "I have something

here you might want to look at."

"You know I can't sing in that contest," I told him. "My voice is so good that everybody else would feel bad!"

Everybody in class laughed with me.

"No, Tonya, this is not for singing. Look at this." He gave me the entry form.

This is what it said. "Drum Contest. Be the Best Drummer. First Prize—One Hundred Dollars."

My heart started to beat fast like drums in a jazz band. But how could I enter that contest? I had no drums. I did not even have any drumsticks.

"I can't do that," I told Mr. Smith.

"Why not?" he asked.

"I don't have any drums."

"You don't need them," he said. "All you need are drumsticks."

"I don't have any drumsticks, either."

Mr. Smith just smiled. He opened a closet in the music room and came back with two brown sticks in his hand. He gave them to me. "Now you do," he said.

CONTESTS
DRUM CONTEST

I held the drumsticks in my hand. They felt smooth and cool. They felt like they could talk. All I had to do was tap them on a table and they would talk the music for me. I didn't need to sing. I had drumsticks.

Do you think Tonya should enter the drumming contest? Why or why not?

4 Facing the Music

I didn't tell my mom about the contest. She would think it was a waste of time. I did not want her to say, "I told you so." So I decided to practice in secret. I wanted to surprise her.

I tapped my new drumsticks on the lunch tables at school, on the back of the bus seats while we were riding home, and on the wooden rails of my back porch at home. I tapped to music in my room when I finished my homework. I did not tap in Ms. Kane's class, though. But it wasn't easy.

Mr. Smith helped me with new beats and new rhythms. He let me practice on the drums in the band room. Those drums were loud and wonderful. My drumsticks made them talk like a room full of powerful animals. My drumsticks knew how to sing on those drums.

The contests were set for Friday after school. The singing contest was in one room. The drumming contest was in another room.

Jackie asked me, "Are you scared?"

"No, not really. But I wish I had my own drums. It's hard to be in a contest where I am the only one who doesn't have drums. Are you scared, Jackie?"

"A little. Most of these kids can sing better than I can," Jackie said as she looked at the other students who had entered the contest.

"You are the best singer in this school!" I told her. "Now go and show them!"

"And you are the best drummer, even without drums!" she told me. She smiled at me and went into the singing room.

I walked to the door of the room where the drumming contest was starting. It was full of boys, boys a lot bigger than I am. And all of them were tapping and rapping with their drumsticks on the drum sets around the room. It was loud and noisy. When I walked in the door, all the noise stopped. A roomful of eyes were on me.

"The singing contest is down the hall," one boy called out.

"I'm not here to sing. I came to play the drums," I said.

All the boys in the room laughed. I said nothing. I got out my drumsticks and sat down. The contest was beginning. I looked at the sign-up sheet. I was going to be the very last drummer.

The first boy got up to play. He said, "My name is Joe. I've been playing the drums for five years."

The music started, and he began to beat the drums to the rhythm. Joe was very good on the drums. He made them talk, but he could not make them sing.

The next boy got up to take his turn. He said, "My name is Rick. I've been playing the drums for six years."

The music started and he began to beat the drums to a smooth and easy rhythm. I knew he could hear the rhythm in his head, just like

I do. I knew he could feel the beat in his fingers, just like I do. I was impressed. Rick could make the drums sing.

The next drummer said, "My name is Roy. I've been playing the drums for seven years."

The music started and Roy struggled to find the beat. He wasn't bad. But he was trying to show off. He acted like he was on TV. Then he dropped his drumsticks. I know he felt bad.

The next drummer said, "My name is Luis. I've been playing the drums for three years."

The music started and Luis found the beat right away. I could tell he loved the music and the drums also. Luis did a very good job.

Finally, it was my turn. I walked slowly to the front of the room. I touched the shiny edges of the drum set with my finger tips.

I said to that roomful of boys, "My name is Tonya. I love drumming." Then I sat down.

The music began. The beat was slow and sad at first, so I touched my drumsticks lightly to the top of the drum. It sounded like a soft rain. Then the music got a little louder and a little faster. I took the sticks and tapped them

CONTEST TODAY

quickly on the drums. I made my drumsticks walk and talk.

Finally, the music got very loud and very fast, like someone running from a wild animal through the jungle. My drumsticks beat wild and powerful as I rapped out the rhythms that I heard.

When the music stopped, the room was very quiet. Some of the boys gave me funny looks. A couple of them smiled. I went outside to sit in the hall and wait for the score from the judges.

I looked up in surprise. Sitting in the hall in a folding chair was my mom.

Why was Tonya surprised to see her mother?

5 And the Winner Is . . .

"What are you doing here, Mom?" I asked.

"Waiting for you," she said. "How did you do in the contest?"

"How did you know about the contest?" I asked. I didn't know what to say. I didn't know how I had done.

"Ms. Kane called me. She told me that Mr. Smith gave you the chance to enter the contest. She also told me that she thinks you have a good chance to win."

"She did?" I was really surprised. "She's my English teacher. She doesn't know much about music. She just knows I get on her nerves." I laughed a little.

"But Mr. Smith is a music teacher. He

knows good music when he hears it. He told me about your drumming. He also thought you had a chance to win."

"He did?" All of this was a big surprise to me.

"So I was thinking that maybe I should give you a chance, too. Maybe I've been wrong about not letting you play the drums."

I could not believe my ears. I could not believe my mother was saying these things. "What about the noise?" I asked.

"Maybe we can work something out," she said.

Jackie came out of the room where the singing contest had been held. She was smiling.

"How did you do?" I asked.

"I don't think I won," she said. "But it sure was exciting! I'll win it next year definitely! How about you?" she asked.

"Some of the guys were very, very good. And all of them had been playing for a long time. But like you said, it was fun!" I said.

The judges came out of the room where the drum contest was held. "We have a winner," they said. "Please come back into the room."

I was shaking. My mom took my hand and we walked in together. I was glad she was there.

"All boys?" she asked me softly as we walked in.

"Yes, all boys," I said. "Maybe you were right. Maybe playing the drums is just for boys."

"Maybe I was wrong," my mother said. "Maybe girls can do anything they want. Maybe it's time the school band had a girl drummer. Maybe it's time for you."

I smiled at my mom. She smiled at me. I could feel my foot tapping out a beat.

The judge spoke. "We have three winners." I held my mom's hand. "The third place winner is Joe." Joe was very happy. He hugged his dad and his mom and collected his prize. He won fifty dollars.

The judge spoke again. "The second place winner is Luis. He wins seventy-five dollars." Luis was really happy, too. I was glad for him.

There was only one winner left. The judge spoke. "The first place winner is . . ." I wanted

to hear my name. I really wanted to hear my name. The judge said, "The first place winner is . . . Rick. He wins one hundred dollars!" Rick jumped from his seat and shouted with joy as he ran to the front of the room to get his prize.

I looked at my mom. I was trying not to be sad, but it was hard. I should have known that I didn't have a chance. All those kids had been playing the drums for a long time. She held my hand and gave me a hug. We started to walk out of the room.

The judge spoke again. "We have one more prize," he said. "For the student who showed the most love of the music and who tried the hardest, we have one more prize. Tonya, will you come to the front, please?"

I looked up in surprise. "Me?" I asked.

"Yes, you," the judge said.

I walked slowly to the front of the room.

"Every year," the judge began, "we bring a set of drums to the contest. And every year we donate that set of drums to the student who shows the most promise."

I looked at my mother. I still did not

understand.

"This year, the judges have decided," he said, "to award this prize to you. The drums aren't new, but they're all yours."

I was so happy, I screamed. All of the boys in the room cheered. They were glad for me. I jumped up and down. I hugged my mom. I kissed the drums. My drums. I was going to make them talk. I was going to make them sing.

I sat down and got out my drumsticks. I touched the cover of the drum gently with the sticks. I could hear the music in my head. Bop-de-bop-bop-bop. Ta-dop. Ta-bop. Ta-dop. Ta-bop. Bop-de-bop-bop-bop. Ta-dop. Ta-bop. Ta-dop. Ta-bop.

I love the beat of my drums.

How do you think Tonya feels about the way the contest turned out?

Meet the Author

I'm a dreamer, a creator, a visionary. I see rainbows where others see only rain, and possibilities when others see only problems.

I'm an author and a poet. I love to write. Words flow from my fingertips, and my heart beats rapidly with excitement as an idea becomes a reality on the paper in front of me.

I'm a teacher. I have always encouraged in my students a love of learning and a desire for excellence. I tell them, "If you want to be a spinner of words, you must first gather them into your heart by reading."

I learned to dream though reading. I learned to create dreams through writing. And I learned to help young dreamers through teaching. I shall always be a dreamer.

To find out more about me and my books, visit my Web site at: **www.sharondraper.com.**

—Sharon M. Draper